Sunshine Seeds

Written and Illustrated by
Sarah Elizabeth Olson

Dedicated to Johnny

Who started the Spread the Sunshine Mission and gave all that he had to spread sunshine and positivity.

As the sun rose over the rolling hills, Mr. Farmer was in the field planting rows and rows of sunflower seeds.

The tractor carefully sowed nice, even rows
of tiny seeds that would soon grow into beautiful, yellow sunflowers.

The sun came up,
the rain poured down
and the tiny seeds grew...

...and grew and grew and grew. They grew until they were tall sunflowers with big yellow faces turning towards the sun. All of the sunflowers were huddled together...all except for one.

Johnny the sunflower stood apart from the rest of the sunflowers. His seed had sprouted and bloomed further down the hill, far from his sunflower family.

Being on his own made Johnny feel
lonely and sad.

As the wind blew and whistled
through Johnny's petals, he
wished he was with the rest of
the sunflowers - safe, secure
and hidden from the wind.

As the wind blew, Bella the butterfly was looking for a safe place to land so she wouldn't be whisked away.

Johnny's petals were the perfect safe place to land.

"Thank you for giving me a safe spot to land!" said Bella to Johnny.

"I am glad you landed here, I am so lonely being apart from the rest of the sunflowers. It is nice to have some company", said Johnny.

"Don't you see?" said Bella, "You helped me find a safe spot to land because you were set apart from the others."

"I wouldn't have found you if you were with the rest of the sunflowers. You are a gift of sunshine and safety!"

As Bella flew away, Bonny the Bee landed on Johnny's disc florets and happily rolled in the fuzzy pollen.

"Thank you for the delicious nectar and pollen! Because you bloomed apart from the other flowers, I reached you first. Now I can use your pollen to pollinate more sunflowers to produce a crop of sunflower seeds and oil. You are a gift of nourishment and sunshine!" said Bonny.

Johnny thought about what Bella the butterfly and Bonny the bee told him. If he hadn't bloomed where he was planted, he wouldn't have been able to help Bella find a safe place to land in the wind, or help Bonny pollinate other flowers.

Johnny started to think of all the other ways he could spread seeds of sunshine to others because of his special spot in the ground...

I can *Serve* by providing a safe place for butterflies and insects to land on my petals.

As Johnny thought about how he could serve, he started to feel

Brighter.

I can *Give* by providing nectar and pollen to pollinators.

As Johnny thought about how he could give, he felt *Sunny*.

I can *Nourish* by feeding people and animals with my sunflower seeds.

As Johnny thought about how he could nourish, he felt *Joyful.*

Johnny was no longer lonely or sad about where he was planted. He realized that his happiness didn't depend on his location or circumstances; it depended on his decision to spread seeds of sunshine in others' lives.

Spreading seeds of sunshine made Johnny feel *Bright, Sunny, Golden, Happy and Joyful.*

No matter where you are planted, you can bloom and spread seeds of sunshine.

You can be Bright, Sunny, Golden, Happy and Joyful.

"So let's not grow tired of doing what is good. At just the right time we will reap a harvest of blessing if we don't give up."
Galatians 6:9

What seeds of sunshine can you give today?

About Johnny and the Spread the Sunshine Mission

Johnny and Sarah Olson and their family

Johnny started the Spread the Sunshine Mission in 2015 as a way to give back to the local communities that he grew up in. Johnny grew up in Minnesota and is an entrepreneur and farmer at heart. Johnny loves to beautify land by planting sunflower seeds and opening the fields to the public once the flowers are in bloom. Johnny's mission is to create a place where people can come and experience peace, hope and healing from the chaos of the world. When people visit the fields of sunshine they experience the warmth of the sun, positivity and joy while surrounded by the bright yellow sunflowers.

Made in the USA
Middletown, DE
10 February 2023

24547646R00015